# The Phantom

# Speaks

I0558870

## or

# More in The Lives

# of

# Chester Knowles

Almost another novel by

Stephen Baum

Illustrated by

Alexandria Skaltsounis

Editor's Note:

The following compilation of notes represents a sequel to the *Memories* section of the novel *One Life or The Lives of Chester Knowles* by Stephen Baum, a Los Angeles author. The notes, which are chronological, were sent to us by a Mr. Howard Hartman, who is the legal representative for the deceased (or perhaps he is just missing) Chester Knowles - as well as for the interests of a Mr. William Miles Morton of Las Vegas, Nevada.

We have no explanation for these notes - nor do we have any reason to print them other than to perhaps entertain the reader. The notes are, indeed, highly unusual. We make no claim whatsoever for their authenticity or veracity, nor do we accept any responsibility for any of the statements made by the supposed Phantom - or by anyone else for that matter.

*Ed.*

This first printing has been financed by a corporate sponsor: *Lone Rangers Inc., P. O Box 424,* Three Rivers, California.

# The Phantom Speaks

April 7, 2011.

I suppose you think that I'm thankful, and that I'm happy and even grateful to have another chance. You know, to write and to talk to you for a while on these pages. In case you are not aware, it is a very significant event for a fictional character, a figment of someone's imagination as it were, to appear in print. It's not an event to be taken lightly. In the world of baseball the equivalent of appearing in print would be to make it to the major leagues: to play for the L.A. Dodgers, the St. Louis Cardinals, the Yankees garshdonnit. It's like pulling one into the left field corner, yanking one down the line. Appearing in print is like a victory trot around the bases! You see, most of us fictional characters are like stuck in the ethereal mist, i.e., the minor leagues forever. So it's definitely a very big deal for a fictional character to appear in print. It's clearly something to be happy about, right? You might even think that for a fictional character like myself an opportunity to appear in print like this is almost like.... Well...... It would almost be like coming to life again.

But that would not be true, would it? Because I am dead! As in D. E. D. I died back there in North Hollywood. Remember? I got shot! That I'm here currently as a phantom to speak with you for any amount of time is something highly improbable by any manner of rational reckoning. So we'll keep it brief.

The key thing - and the thing I want y'all to remember - is that this here book is a work of fiction. Fiction with a capital F, i.e., a work of the imagination. And not only that! It's the work of imagination of a character who is himself imaginary! Fictional on top of fictional. Got it? Thus, any similarity these notes might have to actual living persons, places, or things would have to be quite unlikely given the range of possibilities available.

In any case - and talking from the viewpoint of a phantom who isn't really here and who is dead to boot - I've been looking at things as I go around. And I've been taking down notes, right? You know, I saw Chester writing down notes all the time when I was with him, so I guess I was introduced to the writing biz that way. And I'd also been marginally involved in that *Memories* book about Chester, if you remember that. So I suppose I just kinda fell into this habit of writing notes.

Currently I have access to a computer keyboard, and don't ask me how a phantom can type - or how I obtained access to a computer and all those kinds of questions.

OK, I'll start with these notes. I call them The Observations of a Phantom. Here goes.

# Love

Love. I heard some biologist say that love is the most powerful and most durable of all the emotional states. Think about it. From an evolutionary standpoint, love serves to attach human beings to each other and link them one to the other. They form friendships, partnerships, family clans, and larger social groups. All of which tend to increase the humans' chances of survival. You know, they hunt together, then they share firewood. They keep each other warm at night. Love has definite survival value.

And love is also the thing that everybody feels compelled to sing about. Love. Love. Love. All those songs! Poems, books, movies, broken hearts, tears! Yatta, yatta, yatta. It goes on and on.

I can't say that I really understand very much about it. Even after all this time, and all these lives, I remain largely in the dark. O.K., I know. Chester told me all about it. Chester was big on the feeling of love. He loved it, if you'll excuse the expression. And most people love it as well. I've noticed that. In fact they treasure love. And they miss it so sorely and painfully when they don't have it (which is most of the time from what I can see). Most people behave as though they are lacking love (whatever love is, we still haven't defined it, at least I haven't) and it seems that the poor things can never get enough of it. It is their fear that would appear to be holding them back, blocking things. Fear inhibits love generally. Fear and Love are almost polar opposites.

As a phantom-like aside, I would say that the key determinant in these matters of love and of psychological health in general seems to be whether or not your momma held you in her arms when you were a baby, whether you felt good about yourself. As it turns out, Chester was lucky; he had a happy childhood. Let me add, in another phantom-like aside, that it happens all too often that a child, a baby, is not loved, coddled, sung to, carried around the house and out in the fields, shared with relatives, read stories to, played with, and told that they are good little boys or girls, etc. etc. It happens all too often that children/babies don't get all that (OK, we'll call it) love. And then these children grow up to become parents themselves. And how can they provide the necessary love to their kids when they themselves are consumed or absorbed, even obsessed with finding love for themselves? Luckily (or, more correctly, as a result of mammalian evolution) babies tend to be cute and irresistible. So things often work out well. It's surprising how often things work out well - despite the odds. We'll get to the evens later.

So everybody's looking for love down there on planet earth. They are. And people will go to all sorts of lengths just for a little hug, a caress, a word of praise, perhaps the promise of a good roll in the sack. Especially for a good roll in the sack. Well, thanks again to the process of evolution, the animal, the organism, is wired to have it (call it love): ah, the embraces, the sex, the release, the pleasure, the peace. The company of another and the security of what they call love. And so needy and/or so deprived are the people down there on planet earth that they are more than willing to accept various and sundry substitutes for love: i.e., the so-called vicarious experiences: rock n' roll revues, TV shows, computer games, glossy photographs of movie stars, and the like. Freud called it sublimation, this moving toward, this branching out, into substitute venues.

In short, what this phantom is saying is that love is something very fundamental to the species. It's quite important. Nothing to sneeze at. I myself, being a phantom, don't understand too much about it, as I said. It's like the Amazon jungle to me. Huge and incomprehensible. From what I read, (that's right, phantoms can read, why not?) according to the schema of raja-yoga, love and the ability to feel for others, to empathize: this energy is centered in the heart, sweet valentine, at the fourth chakra - a spiritual step up (but only one step up!) from the more "animal" centers of appetite and domination.

But, like I say, as a phantom, love is just something that's out there. It's a part of the world - just like everything else. It's out there. It's in your heart, as they say. And it's out there too.

## More on Love

I've heard a lot of things said about love while I've been visiting down on earth. You see, I'm an eavesdropper, a peeping-Tom phantom. I soak it all in. And like I said, I have no money riding on this. It's just a phantom's sporting interest. So anyway, as a phantom you hear lots of things, tons of things, zillions of things, said about love - much of it wrapped in romantic ribbons, clever rhymes, haunting melodies, philosophical musings, moonlight magic, and all the rest. For a phantom, it's difficult to separate the wheat from the chaff. You simply hear so much that you don't know what to think.

For instance, they say "Love conquers all". Everybody always says that one.
"Love is all you need". The Beatles said that. Then, "Love, love me do". That was the Beatles again. "You can't hurry love you

just have to wait". That was the Supremes. They say "God is love". That was some church. They say "Love is a Many Splendored Thing", whatever that means, and "Love is All I Need". I think the best one was "Love, Love me do"

Then you have the psychologists, who really don't have a lot to say about the subject. They don't address the issue. In their analytical way they've broken the whole love package into smaller parcels that they can talk about: terms such as security, trust, bonding, attachment etc. But they just assume everyone knows what love is. An interesting omission on their part.

Ah, the poets. They've been on the mark at times. The novelists for sure. Tolstoy talked about love so brilliantly. The *roman*, the novel, of course, concerns a love affair. Well, art is really something else, you know? .... It's just that the humans sing so beautifully sometimes. Those people down there on earth!

Ya gotta love 'em.

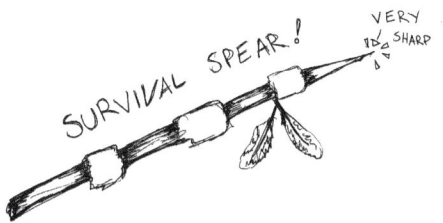

## Survival

Everyone talks about survival. The impetus to stay alive. The urge to keep on living. It's an imperative of the life force. We act, and everything is directed somehow toward staying alive. It's a beautiful mechanism that evolved very early on: all the things of life blossom forth from it. The protoplasm replicates itself. The desire to live... well, it moves all the creatures and organisms. It pre-dates the DNA molecule. It creates the history of the species. Etc, etc, etc.

Surely the people on earth are lucky for their brief chance at being alive. However, few of them seem to realize their good fortune. On a physical level, we are talking about the astonishingly improbable coalescence in space and time of billions of molecules from all over this vast universe - all to create a living being at a certain point in time: an individual organism, an incarnation. And to top it off, a living, walking-upright creature that has seemingly evolved the ability, or at least the potential, to be aware of his or her own self and to perceive his or her own place in this vast universe during a brief moment of life.

With their budding consciousnesses, human beings do occasionally exhibit signs that they appreciate and even savor the experience of being alive. Quite often you see them being nice to each other, which is surely an interesting phenomenon. And certainly they fight extremely hard at times simply to keep the breath of life inside of their corporeal selves. Nobody wants to die. That's a fact. Take it from me. I been there, done that.

Indeed, it looks sometimes as if humans have a stronger - even a qualitatively different - survival "instinct" than those of the other species. Their human consciousness seems to give them an extra edge. Here, I must mention that this phantom has had the opportunity - when he was with Chester Knowles as well as when he was with Tony Santos - to see filmed recordings of elephants playing in the water.

You should have seen them, the big babies. They looked so happy and joyful that even a phantom could recognize it. The same for seals and dolphins, even dogs. It looks like they have a real sense of joy in this world too.

We are all brothers and sisters on this great planet. You'd think that by now the humans would have acquired enough intelligence to stop killing and destroying themselves, as well as destroying and extincting all the other creatures on the earth. Not to mention befouling the air and water and just making a God-awful mess with their drills and explosives - scratching and gouging out the earth's surface, searching for gold. They even talk about things like economic development, mortgage rates, and global strategies. But no, they, the "people" down there are basically a stupid bunch. Really, stupid is the only word for it. And they actually seem to be getting stupider and stupider over time. And yes, I know my grammar isn't always so perfect. But the people down there, they sure are stupid. And they don't appear to be anywhere near ready to turn away from their destructive ways. It's already the 21$^{st}$ century, by gosh. As a phantom, I'm not personally affected. Mine is purely a sporting interest, as I say.

# On the Beach

Yes, I'm on the beach. This is something I share with Chester. That is to say we share this predilection, it's a shared piece of something else. And that shared piece goes a long way toward explaining what this phantom business is all about. But I'll leave that for you to figure out and fill in the blanks.

Sometimes it's just the way that a flock of birds sweeps over the water. Then you are somehow struck by the lines, the curves of the waves. The way the breakers rush in and scurry across the sands. The sound. The wind. The ocean mist. And above all: a sensation of power. It's the force, the energy of this world. It's a force that is everpresent and in all things as far as this phantom can tell. You can feel all that at the beach.

Sometimes I see Chester down here. A co-incidental meeting. Not an accidental meeting. There's a reason why we're both here at the same time. At the beach, I mean. Chester says he likes to come down to the beach to think. Poor guy, even though he's dead, he still likes to think about things - to try to understand them. Poor guy is mostly wasting his time. But all the same, he does have enough sense to come down to the beach. Ya gotta grant him that. Sometimes he watches the pelicans gliding on the wind currents and tries to understand how they know how to fly. He watches the waves breaking and tries to apprehend the physics of wave motion. Those kinds of thoughts are always running through his mind: mathematical musings, the great questions of science and the like. I suppose he's right about that. It would obviously be another form of beauty, a very pure and abstract form of beauty. Sort of a distillation of it all.

But me? I never went in for that sort of thing. Because, for me, it all boils down to the same thing: You're here and then you're gone.

So Chester observes, he takes notes, poor bugger. But he senses the energy, the flow, the rhythm of the waves and the sky and the earth just the same. And he feels the energy of his own self, which of course is the same thing again.

Yesterday, down on the beach, he wades into the water. I yelled to him, "Stupid! You don't even have a body anymore! What are you doing going into the water?"

Chester just smiled at me and kept walking in. I must say, he got met by one of those huge, humongous, crashing waves. What did he do? He dove straight in. Came out on the other side doing a breast stroke. I don't know how he does it. I mean, to swim without a body.

There are a lot of things that we phantoms don't understand. Lots of things. You know, just because we're dead doesn't make us any smarter. Other phantoms - and there are lots of us - may be more clever and certainly many are much wiser than I. But I will tell you this: There are no great, secret, unlock-the-puzzle-of-the-universe kinds of explanations out there in this world. I know that much.

Chester's brother Stan used to say "Everybody's smart. Everybody's stupid", and whenever Chester used that expression, I didn't quite understand his meaning. And I used to ponder over it a bit. You know, how he meant it. Was it supposed to be a statement of truth? Was it intended as cynical? Was it just being cute? You see, as a phantom I didn't understand all these nuances, these idioms, these manners of speech. It takes a while, even for a phantom, to learn all these little tricks. In fact it keeps a phantom young - or ageless if you like. Well, at the least it keeps him very busy - learning all these new things all the time - especially when you consider that a phantom can have multiple lives to live through. Figure it out. Add it up. It just ain't easy. It's a lot of work.

I only mention these less glamorous aspects of phantom life just in case any one reading these notes actually feels jealous of Chester and myself, or is envious of our phantom status. They might think it's cool to be a phantom. You know, to move around, float in the air, go to the beach. I tell them all: "Just live the life you have. Eat everything on the plate". That's what I say. You never can tell what will happen. I tell them that too.

# Food

Does a phantom eat? "Why not?" I say. I mean, even if we only appear - or rather, even though we are visible in the flesh like human beings for quite brief periods of time relatively speaking - all the same we phantoms do try to maximize our opportunities and to enjoy ourselves while we can. And that's good advice all around.

There's an expression in baseball - yes, phantoms have a thing for baseball. We're kind of drawn to all things beautiful, you know. Anyhow, they say that when a player gets to play in the Major Leagues - but for only a few games, and then gets sent back down to the minors - that he was up there "for a cup of coffee".

So what I'm getting at is that, personally, I haven't had the good fortune to sample all the foods from all over the world. Time - despite everything we might think about it - is not an infinite dimension. Opportunities, even for a phantom, are limited. That's the nature of the world. Phantoms can't do anything about that. So, making the best of the situation, I do enjoy a hearty meal, a nice, dry wine. Say, why not a cigarette and an aperitif? And a good cup of coffee of course, as I was saying.

This phantom is a vegetarian however. "Do no harm". That's the first rule of medical practice. You know, if the people on the earth would eat grains directly instead of growing grain to feed cattle and then slaughtering all the cattle to make hamburgers, then there would be enough food for all. They wouldn't be worrying about their cholesterol levels, either. People would live longer. Not to mention the cattle.

So I figure - without getting too moralistic about it - that the simplest thing to do while you're living on this earth is just to do your best and try to not make things worse for everybody and everything else.

I try to keep my so-called carbon footprint as light as possible - which for a phantom might not be so fantastic a trick, I admit. After all, we're not very heavy or corporeal most of the time. But heck, it ain't my fault that I'm a phantom.

# Phantom R&R

What, you ask, is rest and relaxation for a phantom? What do we phantoms do for fun? Or, rather, do we have any fun at all? That's a question too. Well, as I was saying earlier in these Observations, much of the time we phantoms are pretty busy just trying to keep up with things. Current events, news of the day, cultural developments and the like. It seems like all the time there are all these new "human species" things to learn. Lots of 'em. Every lifetime you have, every new person you receive, every situation, etc., you have to learn the languages, dialects, customs, etc. All from scratch! It's a lot of work.

The lucky thing for us phantoms is that - if you're lucky - and if you put in some time with your person, say Chester Knowles for instance... well, after a while that person can learn to pretty much manage on his or her own. Like I say, in these matters you need a lot of luck. Tony Santos, for instance, required a lot of time, a lot of work. But, as I was explaining, if you can get the person to be on a straight path, to take care of themselves, and to be able to manage on their own for a while, well then, as a phantom, you are free to set off on your own. You know, come down to the beach. Or go downtown. Whatever.

As you already know, I, as a phantom, enjoy a good meal and the fine cigar. And quite a good number of the so-called worldly pleasures. Intimacy, romance. Ah, the feeling of falling in love. The love-making in the night. It's just great. Then there are the ballgames, the hikes in the mountains, the beach of course. Yeah, we phantoms are very capable of having a good, sweet time when we like. I'll let you in on a little professional secret: a good phantom can even have a good time when he's inside someone else's body, like Chester's for instance, or even Willie's.

While we're on the topic of Willie, I think Willie is now aware of my presence. For a long time he confused me with Chester, which was quite natural of course, but by now he is clearly aware that I am a spirit that is with him sometimes. He keeps it to himself, Willie does. He doesn't try to understand it all, and doesn't work himself into a lather about it all - the way Chester used to do. You know, Chester used to try to figure everything out all the time. But Willie's different. Willie has good common sense. And if he reads this, as I imagine he eventually will, let him take my blessing. My hat's off to him for how he's been doing so far, and all my best wishes to him for his continued success. And if he ever needs me, he knows where to find me. It's like that Four Tops song, Willie: "Reach Out, I'll Be There".

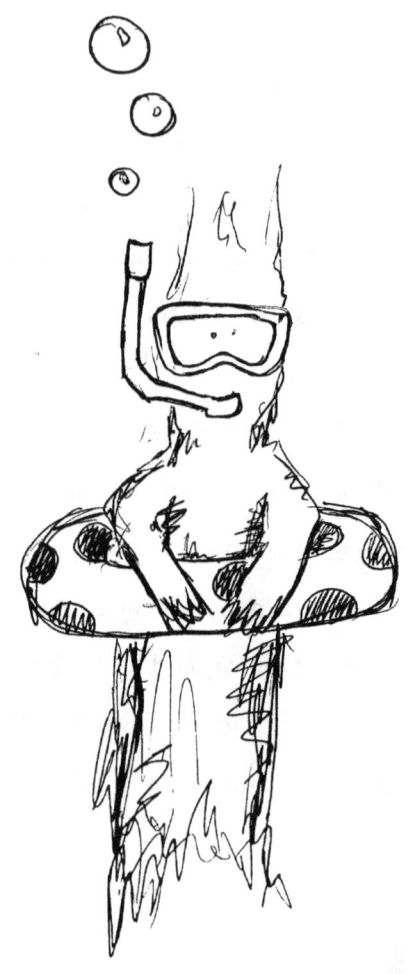

# On the Beach

I'm on the beach again. Don't believe me? Look.

OK, so how does a phantom get to materialize on the beach?
I don't know how I do it myself, to tell you the truth. Certainly
there are phantoms who understand the mechanics and
dynamics, etc, etc, of out-of-body time travel. And there are
even phantoms that can do transmission work on
reincarnation and eternity. But I am definitely not one of
them. All I can tell you is that I took the bus. Found a seat in
the back and rode out to the beach. It was pretty simple.
Even for a phantom.

The ocean mist, borne by the high wind, bathes my phantom
face. The movement - the power - of this tiny piece of the
world, this piece of fringe of the great ocean - floods my
phantom senses. And, I tell ya, it feels great, even for a
phantom.

Chester's not here today. But Howard's here- or rather he will be. Howard Hartman, that's Chester's friend, if you remember. Howard is Willie Morton's friend too. Howard knows all about Chester and Willie, and he even knows a bit about me. Howard represents me in all legal matters, by the way.

I'm going to be giving him these notes, these *Confessions and Whatnots of a Phantom,* these *Observations*. He'll get them published for me. I don't know if I need to remind you, but as a fictional character I need help with some of the practicalities of - excuse the expression - life, and Howard has always been very helpful. If you're reading this then I guess he succeeded. I tell ya, Howard is a good kid.

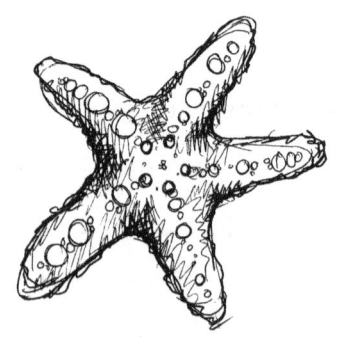

# Howard Speaks

April 29, 2011.

I received these notes from Chester. I found them on the beach. They were in a three-ring binder, wrapped in a brown paper bag and tied with a string.

Chester's calling himself the phantom now. No matter. I understand that he needs a lot of space to operate. He's asking me to publish these notes, which as you can see, I am doing.

It was interesting that I was at the ocean at all. I had been thinking about Chester all day for some reason. Of course I hadn't seen Chester in a long time, like maybe fourteen years or fifteen years. Anyhow, on a whim, I made a slight detour in my plans, and I parked my car on the shoulder of the PCH. Just to get out and stretch. You know, just to take a walk on the shoreline. I felt I needed to. And, what do you know? Well, you *do* know. I found these notes.

I must say, it looks like Chester has gone out on a limb with this one. He thinks he's being clever or funny. But, from what I can tell, it's just irrational. Especially the part about being a phantom.

If Chester taught me anything, it's that it has to be rational, i.e., to make sense. From a logical standpoint it has to be at least possible. So, if someone tells you something, it has to hold up to rational scrutiny. That's to say: consistent with sense experience and with what you perceive.

Oh, I know that the Phantom/Chester is in another world. And that the world he is in is obviously a world beyond our immediate senses. And beyond our understanding. Almost by definition it's beyond our understanding!

So, I shouldn't even be trying.

"Just accept it all. Eat what's on your plate," Chester told me. He's right of course.

He instructed me, by the way, to publish these notes. There was a letter scotch-taped to the cover of the folder. It stated (and I quote).

*Howard,*

*I see that you found these notes. I'll give you more "Observations of a Phantom" every now and then. I'll just leave them out for you on the beach - like I did today. You'll publish them when I'm done - or whenever I'm out of these blank notebooks, whichever comes first.*

*Thanks a lot, Howard. And all the best.*

*Signed*

*The Phantom*

*P.S. Regards from Chester*

So, that's what I'm going to do. The remainder of this book will be these notes: The *Observations of a Phantom*.

The text will be interspersed, however, by interpretive and professional-sounding comments by yours truly, Howard Hartman, because I have discovered (if you don't already know it) that it's fun to write in these books and it's also fun to try to figure things out, and to carry on this crazy Chester Knowles thing. And just to remind you, in case you forgot, I'm a fictional character too. Good Luck.

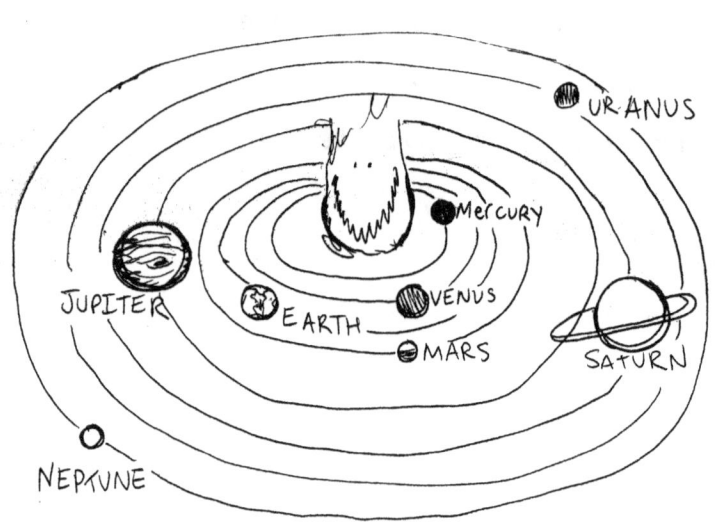

# The Phantom  Speaks Again

(regarding matters of science and the

finding of universal laws)

# Phantom Observations

*"You don't know what you're doing…. Well, you know what you're doing, but you don't know why."*

This Phantom overheard that admonishment, that little lecture, delivered by a 40 year-old to a 30 year-old. They were standing outside an office building, and I was walking - or passing by shall we say.

What presumption! To think you can understand the *why!* The *what* is hard enough. Even for a phantom. Barely anyone down on the earth really knows what is happening. Not even that Stephen Hawkings guy! Virtually nobody I've met in my various travels - human, phantom, or otherwise - seems to know what is really going on with all the sub-atomic particles/probability fields in our little universe. Not to mention alternative arrangements of energy and matter in other places or realms that probably - or almost surely - do exist.

So, as I say, knowing what's what is good enough. He should have let it go at that.

# On the Apple Falling
# on Sir Isaac Newton's Head

Gravitation. What is it? One thing falling toward another. Pulled. Why? Who the heck knows? How? Answer: With a force in universal accordance with the equation

$F = m_1m_2/distance^2$.

OK, that's it on Gravitation. The equation says it all. Nothing more to say.

At least until Einstein came along.

∞∞∞∞∞∞∞∞∞∞∞∞∞∞∞∞∞∞∞∞∞∞∞∞∞∞∞∞∞∞∞∞∞∞

# On E=mc2

A correction to, a conceptual adjustment of Newton's Law of Gravitation. You see, Einstein figured that Newton's laws must always be correct - universally and for all times and places. His trust in the overriding power of the universal laws was his genius. So Einstein adjusted our conceptions of time and space so that the laws could remain universal.

$E=mc^2$. Think about it. The equivalence of matter and energy! It gives you kind of a fresh perspective on things. At least for a phantom it does. You know, something to just think about.

∞∞∞∞∞∞∞∞∞∞∞∞∞∞∞∞∞∞∞∞∞∞∞∞∞∞∞∞∞∞∞∞∞∞∞∞∞∞

# On Heisenberg's Uncertainty Principle and Quantum Mechanics

*(Obviously these observations and explications of a phantom are not for the scientific community or for anyone who knows any better)*

I don't care what you say. It's hard to be in two places at the same time. I'm a phantom and I can't do it. You have to remember, though, that the sensory apparatus of humans, which has evolved and specialized over the years for the picking of wild berries and the smashing in of skulls... well, that sensory apparatus is obviously circumscribed. And these neuro-sensory systems that have evolved only pick up a small part of the energy out there in the physical world. We (and again forgive the use of the word we) see and "our" human bodies have evolved with seeing in mind (to wit, the large, convoluted ocular lobes). And we receive, we perceive, (sorry about all the "we's") only the ROY G. BIV spectrum - the "visible" light quadrant of the electromagnetic spectrum. The other wavelengths are undetected, invisible. We're limited, as I say. Our thinking, our rationality is similarly restricted. We're not so smart. And necessarily so. Items and activities that are not survival necessities have been screened out over the years via natural selection. We're designed to hunt, gather berries, raise children mostly. But we've also been given, or have actually developed as a survival tool, the ability to think rationally and the curiosity to go along with it. It's a Cro-Magnum thing most likely. Larger groupings of primates became possible as soon as rationality, and language too, began to develop.

Our ancestors began to look at the stars. And to ask questions. And they discovered mathematics. And mathematics is universal. If it's true, it's true all over. If you follow the math, it has to be correct. That's what they say. And it really *is* true, as far as this phantom can determine. Eventually, they'll get to some Grand Unified Theory. The G.U.T. And, finally, at long last, Relativity and Quantum

Mechanics will be united in one elegant equation or two. They'll have explained everything. But I'll bet'cha that even then they won't have explained everything. Because before you know it, they'll discover something else - some additional realms or heretofore hidden dimensions to our universe. Something probably right under our noses! And it'll be back to square one in terms of figuring everything out. I'll lay you even money.

# Politics and History

OK. Politics. History. Let's talk about it. Political Science. Natural History. Again, the thing is to find the laws. The Universals. Up to now, the best the social sciences have been able to do is to talk in terms of probabilities. You know: Most of the people most of the times, except for when such and such, and also taking into account….yatta, yatta, yatta. The early sociologists searched for laws. Durheim, Marx. But, despite all their ardent and sincere efforts, the sociologists, the political scientists, the historians have yet to come up with anything like Newton: rigorous laws of human behavior and history that are sufficient, universal, and (OK, I'll say it) elegant.

Marx's law of economic determinism is a good stab at it. It's quite true: money makes the world go round. It's a pretty good handle on economics and politics/history. A decent handle on everything. Show me the money. But his description of the food chain, the dialectic of class struggle doesn't really play out. Nowadays, in America at least, class consciousness is largely absent. Why is that? They all like to call themselves middle class in America. What happened to the struggle, the class awareness? Apparently Marx didn't fully appreciate how stupid most people are. To quote P.T. Barnum, "There's a sucker born every minute". To quote Paul Simon, "They think they're gliding down the highway when in fact they're slip-sliding away".

Looking at it from a phantom's historical perspective, I've seen it all before. I mean, to send young soldiers off to die and to fill their heads with all kinds of bullshit (excuse the expression) is a very old game. I guess it would have to be called a universal. Likewise, "taking as much money and as much land as you can for as long as you can" is also a very old game. The game of the kings! They're still playing it. Nothing new there.

At times it looks to this phantom as if the whole human race down there is simply going down the tubes. You know, racing toward their own destruction. They're just messing up the world so badly that soon much of the land will be unfit for even human habitation. Talk about blowing a good thing!

But, never worry. The processes of evolution will forge a new world, a new kind of ecosphere. There'll be a different world: one without horses, apples, wine, and probably without too many people (which I suppose is just as well). Eventually the earth, our beloved blue orb, will heal itself, forget the wrongs done by the humans, and eventually wobble its way into a new and probably a cooler orbit for an eon or two.

Like I say, this phantom has what can only be called a sporting interest in these matters. If you wanted me to put down any real money on the future of humanity on planet earth, you'd have to give me heavy odds.

# The Phantom on Sports

OK, let's get spiritual. There is, you know, a spirit on the face of the waters. In fact, there are lots of them. All around. Call it a spirit world, call it the Divine Presence, call it the Omnipresence. Call it what you will, but something is out there.

And, as a phantom, I tend to look - indeed I tend to actively search - for evidence and manifestations, if you will, of the spirit. And the manifestations are everywhere. Ya can't miss 'em. Really.

In today's world, even on TV (and I suppose TV does represent today's world as well as anything else I can think of) the sports arena, the baseball diamond, the basketball court are some of the best places to look for the Spirit. That's why I mention it. Because even if they wrap the sports up in multiple layers of taped replays, promos, commercials, and endless commentary/chatter, etc., etc., the spirit - the brave spirit of the human species inevitably comes shining through.

It's a great thing, and you can see it all the time. Especially on the playing field. Ah, the glory of the champion as he crosses the finish line, arms upraised. Then, too, there's the sportsman's grace in defeat. His extra effort, his hustle. The warrior spirit. The beauty of a double play, a good bounce pass, a soaring ski jump, a slam dunk, a close play at the plate, a reverse lay-up.

They're all beautiful things. And what, I ask you, is beauty, anyway?

It's all just the spirit, the identification with it, and it's all in front of you. All the time. Eat what's on your plate. Open your eyes, that's what I say.

The difficulty with being a phantom, I suppose, is that your eyes are open nearly all the time. Never a dull moment for a phantom. No rest for the weary. Because a phantom in his or her brain and in his or her heart of hearts also knows that he or she is a lucky happenstance, a fortuitous coalescence of myriads of large molecules and events - living events - all for a brief moment. That moment can appear endless. But it isn't. A phantom is here, and then he's gone too.

# On Loneliness

You might think a phantom would know close to nothing about loneliness. You'd think that being a part of the so-called "immaterial" whole, the great vastness (the whole enchilada) would be sufficient on a psychological level for an ethereal being such as myself. But we phantoms get lonely, too. Even a phantom enjoys a friendly smile, a hand to hold, a lover, a warm body in the night. We phantoms like it too. It's nice.

Certainly everybody's favorite social activity, and one of the most popular of the social magnets down there on earth is the "warm body in the night friend". You might think it strange for a phantom to be talking about sex, but what can I tell you? We like it too. It's that good! It's what you would call a flower of the evolutionary process (forgive the closeness of the metaphor). Some of my best times on earth as Tony, Chester, Willie and the rest (yes, there were others) were spent in this way. And I mention the sex because it's related to the loneliness subject.

You see, over time, different species have evolved very different sexual behaviors. And the sexual behaviors in each species are highly correlated to the other social behaviors. That's to say they're closely related to, and surely genetically linked and/or contiguous on the chromosome to....well, you know what I mean. Sex is tied in very closely to the social behaviors. You have herd animals, the zebras and the bison, grazing out on the great plains. Yes, and lone wolves prowling the steep and rocky mountainsides. You have sea turtles plumbing the depths of the blue. You have rabbits, birds, fishes, snakes, kangaroos, etc., etc.

Well, for each species the courtship and sexual behaviors are quite different. But we humans (OK, I call myself a human. I say *we* humans, etc. but it's only as a manner of speech. How else am I supposed to talk?). Well, "we" have taken sex to another level. We've turned sex into a year-round, all-seasons-are-OK, face-your-partner, help me make it through the night, long-weekend-in-the-Poconos jamboree. And, I say, it's all part and parcel of what you can only call a general trait of "social gravitation": a tendency to seek out others: to avoid and to dislike loneliness. It's a sort of evolutionary insurance policy. We don't like to be alone for too long. Consequently, in order to induce us to have social relationships (and thereby increase our chances of survival), there have evolved mechanisms or magnets to pull us in. These "socially magnetic" behaviors, many of them complex and highly evolved, have been favored by natural selection. That's why we see them, right? Well, nearly all of these inherited behavior patterns discourage being alone.

There's what they call friendship, even love. Then there are all sorts of games, fighting behaviors, group memberships, clubs, gangs, team work, even bureaucracies. And then all that happy, "belonging" stuff they all talk about nowadays. There's probably an actual gene complex for "belonging". Initially you "belong" to your mother and to your family, then you belong to a tribe, later to a nation or an empire. Or to the entire universe! Actually, being a part, feeling a part of a group, can be the first step toward realizing that we are part of something that is greater than our immediate selves. One might even experience an identification with that larger universal symphony, that great OM that's humming all around us.

So what's interesting (actually it's more problematic than interesting) is that this feeling of belongingness to a tribe or nation generally functions to bind the individual, and to make him or her a "useful member of society". That same centrifugal force, that "social instinct", tends to keep him or her away from the fringes and to distance his or her self from the realization that he or she is a living part of the universe and of everybody. And that he or she is not really alone at all. There was no reason to feel lonely in the first place.

But overall, people can't tolerate loneliness. If you look down on earth today, you'll see millions of people talking on telephones, computers, headsets, as well as on a host of other little telephone-type kinds of devices and thingies. They type, they text, they "network". They leave messages for each other on little slivers of silicon. It's pathetic-looking to a phantom. The people think that they escape loneliness. But they don't of course. Simply, there are fewer and fewer individuals who are able to tolerate loneliness. The paradox is that it is precisely those occasional and isolated, lonely individuals - those who are able to tolerate loneliness: those prophets in the desert, those lone wolf mathematicians, those saints and sinners who've "seen the light" - it is those lonely spirits who can occasionally, and very occasionally as far as I can tell, come to realize their identity with the whole, the whole enchilada, I mean. So, I guess a little loneliness is a good thing sometimes. All the same, speaking for myself, even as a phantom, I still like the warm body in the night.

May 14, 2011

## Howard Makes an Entry

OK, I just want to inform you that the notes stopped at that point. I am giving these notes to Willie, who, for reasons that are plain and obvious, is the one who should continue this story.

Signed

*Howard Hartman*

Howard Hartman

THE PHANTOM,
PHANTOM
MENACE

May 20, 2011

## Willie Morton Speaks

Howard just presented me with this notebook of Chester's. He told me to read it, and he said that I should write in it too - just like in the other book. Now, exactly how Chester gives this notebook to him, Howard, is a good question. After all, Chester is dead. But Howard says that he's been going down to some beach in Malibu, CA and he just finds them there - these notes - bound in a dirty old 3-ring binder that is sitting on my desk right now. The binder holds two spiral notebooks full of "Observations". They're signed by someone called the Phantom - which was a name Chester liked to use for himself. But it could be anybody. It's easy to pull the wool over Howard's eyes.

Yet Howard thinks that this Phantom really is Chester, and now that I've read it, I can see what he means. Howard has a point. This Phantom is definitely someone tied in to the whole business with Tony, Chester, and myself. Like it's all just one big thing: One Life, One Universe, one great story about nothing. "A tale told by an idiot, signifying nothing".

Hey, Hey. It's all just one big thing. I get it. It's just there. And the way I figure it, why get so excited about it all the time?

Anyhow, what I assume would be my official responsibility in this situation, my duty to do right now is to try to fill you in on what's been going on since we last spoke - or wrote. Or whatever. What I mean is everything that's happened since the last book. It's been a long time. Fifteen years or thereabouts. I believe it was in Chester's so-called Memories section that we last spoke (Well, we didn't speak literally, but in a literary kind of way we had a sort of conversation. And if you can figure that one out, you're pretty good).

There's been a lot of water pass under the bridge. A lot of things have happened. Chester, of course, died. Let's not forget that, and let's not have a discussion on it either! He's dead. Chester is dead. His band, our band, the Lone Rangers, pretty much broke up about a year after that, although some of us did stay together for a while in Vegas. Actually we had plenty of gigs. But without Chester it wasn't the same. Also, Davy died. We were all crushed by that, myself most of all. I still miss the old fat man.

Anyhow, later on, a good couple of years later on.... Well, me, Gene, Howard, and Jackson the guitarist, and some of his friends, well, we got it going again. And we're still playin'. We've kept it goin'. We still enjoy playing, and we're still doin' it.

Howard left Vegas and wound up staying with Andrea in Los Angeles. Eventually he married her and they have three kids now, ages seven and five, and three. Somethin' like that. Real nice kids. Howard's old flame, Natale, remember her? Well, she's still in Vegas. She got married too - to some guy I don't know. She became a director of some private psycho-therapy and substance abuse center business, which, last I heard, is apparently in some kind of legal trouble. Poor Natale, she used to come by occasionally to hear us play when we had gigs in Vegas. She used to say that our music reminded her of Chester. Then she would start to cry. But, as I started to say, we're not in Vegas too much anymore. Most of the time we're down in Phoenix, and around Flagstaff. Also near Sedona, up and down highway 37, and around that neck of the woods. Nice country. And when we have work it's great. Just me and Gene and a new drummer called Milton. Sometime a local sits in with us. Gene has musician friends all over Arizona.

So, we're still playing music: Gene, me, Milton, and the others. Like the great Willie Nelson said, "We're on the road again". Ha, Ha. It ain't a bad life, you know, playing music. But, I mean, you never put down roots anywhere. "I was born a rambin' man". Hank said that. It seems I'm just kind of wired to do it: play music, be on the road. For me it's a gesture of love and respect for the spirit of Tony and his dream. And to Chester, too. To keep it all going. But as far as this Phantom character is concerned, I'm not too sure. I'm not sure if he's a remaining piece of Chester, or if he's somebody or something else that's new altogether. But on with the show. I'm giving this notebook back to Howard. And if he never asks me again to write anything in it, that'll be too soon for me.

July 12, 2011

# Howard's Introduction

### to the next installment of

### Phantom Observations

OK, I promise to keep this short. Famous last words.

Anyway, Willie returned the binder and the notebooks to me last month. Willie surely is a reluctant writer, especially for a fictional character. Most of us are pretty chatty. So, to return to the matter at hand, i.e., these Observations of a Phantom or whatever they are, a number of weeks have passed. Actually, to tell you the truth, I pretty much had forgotten all about these notes, as I was quite busy at work etc, etc. That's just how it is.

But now I've received another installment of "Observations" and clever sayings from the Phantom. Once again he left them for me on the beach. They were wrapped neatly this time in a parcel made from a paper bag. They were lying right near the shoreline but they were nice and dry. So, they couldn't have been sitting there very long, right?

However, there was nobody around in the vicinity. And no footprints. I looked up and down the beach. It was early in the morning and no one was there.

Don't ask me what I was doing driving on the PCH early on a Wednesday morning. That's a long story, and it's not really that interesting I don't think. Anyway, here are the notes - which, as you can see, I have copied (word for word, I swear it's all verbatim) onto my laptop, and which are now in hard-copy print. But as you are reading this I suppose I didn't have to tell you that, did I?

OK, here's the next installment of the Phantom Speaks - or whatever Chester, or the Phantom, wants to call this thing.

# The Phantom on Going Fast

Let's talk about the speed of light. Contemplation on light got Einstein going. Newton too. Well, it just appears to be a constant in our universe at 186,000 miles per second, or 300,000 km/sec. That's pretty fast, buddy. Too fast for us humans (excuse me again for the use of the "us" in the "us humans" expression, but some habits are hard to break). In any case, the speed of light is too fast for "us" to grasp. Neither/nor to wrap "our" little brains around. However, the speed of light is the going rate, the operational speed for most phenomena, that's to say for 99% of all the "known" particles/waves/string vibrations/etc. in the universe. It's the universally constant, same-wherever-you-look velocity of light waves, radio waves, x-rays, electricity, not to mention all the other sub-atomic particles/waves/vibrations which comprise our busy universe - including us. It's the measure of all the goings-on that are going on inside the atoms and molecules that are coursing through our brains and bloodstreams. Everything's zipping around at the speed of light, or something like it.

It's just our minds, our mental processes that are as slow as the proverbial molasses on a cold day (I think it's molasses that they say). Even inside our knotty brains, within our dopamine-bathed dendrites and neuro-synapses, the electrons are flying, hopping here and there to keep us sane or crazy as the case may be. Molecules are transforming, reproducing, toying with their electrical charges - and all this business, official and unofficial, is being conducted at lightning speed. So forget about the 60 mph speed limit. The going rate for light is 669,600,000 mph. Like I say, hold on to your hat.

# The Phantom Takes a Sentimental Stroll Down Hollywood Boulevard

I suppose you know by now that I've been visiting and living with various fictional characters who live in the Los Angeles area. And for a good while now. Actually, ever since Tony first came out here. And, as an official Phantom, I like to keep abreast of things. You know, to follow the fashions, to study developments on the political front etc, etc. And also to make bets. I confess: I'm a bit of a gambler. I bet on election results, the ball games of course, and even on things like the chances for human survival and salvation. I have my finger in quite a number of pies. That's why I watch Hollywood. Because that's what people are buying now: Entertainment. A place to be, to hang out, just something to do. So I watch what's going on in Tinseltown, Lalaland, LA .

From what I can tell, they've had the so-called Hollywood stars stuff from the very beginning of the movie biz. Nearly one hundred years. But this celebrity stuff I've been observing recently is something different. It's - how do they say it? - over the top? This fascination, this identification, this deification of Hollywood movie stars.

Naturally, idol worship is not a new phenomenon. The people on earth have been adoring their local heroes, their patron saints and the like, marching in midnight processions and masses, and dancing around the ol' bonfires to celebrate and honor the great nature gods for quite a long time now. But the old gods were local; they were family protectors. They were tribal gods, and they connected to something real. But now we (again, excuse the "we") have TV celebrities, and we have our favorite stars and personalities on an assortment of video screens. And everyone is hoping for his or her own fifteen minutes of fame and glory.

Today you can see them crowding the *Starwalk* on Hollywood Boulevard in Los Angeles like pilgrims flocking to the Holy Waters of Lourdes. They gossip about television and movie actors and all sorts of other individuals they have never met in real life just like the washerwomen of centuries past used to talk about their neighbors.

That's another universal by the way: gossiping. People always did it. Always will. The more negative, the better they like it.

Gossip's basically a catty, back-biting, hostile sort of activity no matter how you cut it. And it's universal. Sorry 'bout that.

Getting back to Hollywood Boulevard, the people, the common people, have never had such quick and such easy in-your-face idols and gods as they do today. And it's nearly a world-wide phenomenon, don't forget. A lot of people are watching the same show.

On Hollywood Boulevard you can see them: lined up and packed in some sort of celluloid brine. Crowding, eager for a glimpse, a vicarious whiff, of what they think is Hollywood glamour - the actual experience of which, of course, turns out to be a heavily perfumed and rather seedy ride later that night.

The universal principle here (because there is one) is the need, the yearning to bask in the glory of an idol, someone or something that is high on a pedestal. The old folk gods have bitten the dust. We (apologies once again for the "we") are left with the TV (or some other piece of technology) playing all the time in the other room.

I suppose one of the "advancements" of modern civilization was the worship in the 19$^{th}$ and 20$^{th}$ centuries of abstract ideas. These ideas, these "isms" temporarily supplanted the religious idols. You know, the great utopian notions: communism, nihilism, pacifism, and all the political and philosophical "isms" that were going to cure all our ills. One can see how well all that stuff turned out! Nonetheless, there was a belief, even an actual identification with something larger than one's self, i.e. the good of society, love of one's neighbor and all that stuff. A noble way to live one's life, I suppose. But, inevitably, it was a dead-end.

Ha, ha. We phantoms can laugh, being dead already.

Anyhow, the old gods have bitten the dust - despite the loud wailings of the Wahabees and the Khumeinee-ites and the all-American religious right wing turn-back-the-clockers. Despite their desperate protests we have new heroes today. Our heroes and gods change seasonally on our screens. Without worshipping them openly, we see their faces everywhere. So much for idle worship.

Republican          Democrat

?

# The Phantom on Politics in America

I'm not sure if at any point in modern history (the past few hundred years) has the large majority of the population ever possessed the cognitive skills necessary to follow a rational argument. You know, the ability to weigh the pros and cons, and to examine and consider evidence, etc. Generally people are "swayed by their emotions" or hooked onto some "belief system". Or just plain stupid. Perhaps the Dutch and some of the European nations have enough educated people to achieve a rational society and democratic government, but most of the time political leaders, kings, and chieftains of various kinds over the years have been able to rouse the emotions of the people whenever necessary and then to sway them in one direction or the other with a load of emotional bullshit.

You wouldn't think it would still work, i.e., that people are that stupid. After all, today the people down there on earth have the internet. They have access, there's all sorts of information available. But nowadays in America, the politicians - including nearly the entire lot of the Republican Party, goshdarnit - have realized that there is no particular need to present the voters/populace with rational proposals, and no need to engage in any rational argument. Negative advertising and even Goebels-style "big lies" (i.e., Obama is a Muslim, Obama is not an American etc), will work on a large segment of the population. Government is evil they tell us. And then they tell us with no obvious shame or embarrassment that they are not the bad guys. Never mind that they have been running things all along. With this weak line of bullshit, as well as a lot of hard cash, they get elected. They lower taxes for their millionaire friends, cut a few sweet deals for themselves, steal all the paper clips and whatever office furniture they can haul, and effectively sell the deed to the farm. Afterwards they can apparently return safely to their Texas homesteads, their pockets well lined and their consciences somehow assuaged by their unshakable "patriotism". And clearly they will keep on pilfering and highway robbering until further notice, or until the people get wise to them. Thus they capitalize on the people's stupidity.

So, until the day that enough people receive a decent enough education (Uh oh. I see one of those Catch-22 things) to see through all their bullshit, there's going to be more of the same. Of course, that day of enlightenment may not arrive very soon, and by then the destruction to our forests, our

(yes, our) land, seas, and minds (yes, minds too. You think all

that TV and texting has no effect?). Well, the damage by then

will probably be irreparable in any case. That's why I said

before that this Phantom is not laying any heavy money on

the future of mankind here on this planet.

But at least they can go down swinging. That's what I say.

# The Phantom Waxes Poetic on the Big Bang

We sure are lucky (or rather, they, the humans) sure are lucky to be present and to be alive and conscious at this current point of time, 2011 C.E. And to be situated at this amazingly comfortable distance from the sun, riding on this blue, lolling, pulsing and geologically alive planet in this very nearly circular orbit. At such and such a time/distance from the Big Bang as well.

Because otherwise we wouldn't be talking right now, would we? Even a phantom wouldn't stand much of a chance in any of those zillion degree-Big Bang particle soups. Conversely, there's no way that any phantom that I know of could ever hope to thrive and/or flourish in any of those Black hole, super-solid, time-erasing, atom-crunching/chowder environments either, for that matter. And talking about matter, why oh why does every particle in the universe feel attracted to all the other particles? What is this gravitational constant anywaze?

Chester tried to explain it to me on more than one occasion, but I never understood it too well, nor did Chester for that matter, I don't think. If the matter is equivalent to the energy/divided by the speed of light squared, then the force, the gravitational constant (of this particular universe, the one we know) is something inherent in the space-time. Likewise, the matter is inherent in the energy - whatever "inherent" means.

So sitting in the garden, feet up, peeking out at a sunny micro-sliver of this revolving orb, even a phantom has to count his lucky stars. You know, just to be here.

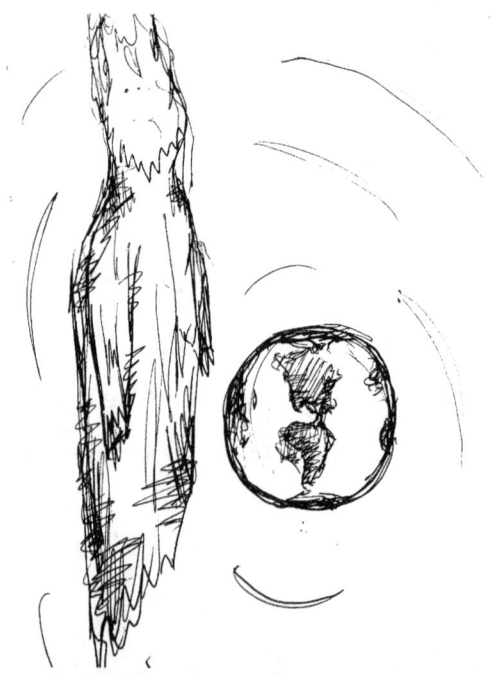

# The Phantom on Thinking

The ability to think while you're doing something else. Only the "higher" primates (and that means "us" human beings and perhaps the occasional introverted orangutan) can do it. That is: to think of one thing while you're doing something else. It's simply not done at all by other animals. I suppose this "higher" mental capacity serves to provide an advantage, a leg up, to the homo sapiens, although I personally think it comes with too high a price-tag. Because any fool will tell you that too much thinking is no good for anybody. Ignorance is bliss and all that.

This recently-evolved human capacity to have multiple thoughts and even to entertain various abstract ideas - and furthermore, to go and erect conceptual frameworks for those ideas (as if the ideas really existed as actual entities), and then even to engage in metaphysical musings, etc, etc. All that over-activity creates neurosis - did I say etc, etc? (ha, ha) - and other forms of mental illness. Doubts, second thoughts, misgivings, regrets, guilt feelings. You know, first you do something and then you feel bad about it afterwards?

The other animals don't do that. They just do one thing at a time. They don't get mixed up and "conflicted". They have horse sense and it's good enough.

All that thinking has created quite a mess down there on planet earth. But maybe they can think their way out of it. Like I say, from my vantage point, it's even money.

June 26, 2011

# Phantom Announcement

I thought I was just being cute when I stated that I'd continue with these observations until I run out of paper. Well, it's happened. Here I am at the end of the notebook. Only a couple of pages left.

So this final chapter is going to have to be a summary. A culmination of this phantom's wisdom, a collection of the hard-earned gleanings of life (lives). This will have to be the cream of the philosophical crop, the choicest of the poetical pickings, a rhapsody of rhyme, time, motion and ...

... Well, let me tell you something, sweet valentine, you're going to be disappointed. This phantom still hasn't gotten even half a handle on nearly anything at all, not to mention the whole messy enchilada. Not one bit. No way. And as for poetic and philosophical, forget about it. What did you think? What were you expecting? Anywaze?

But to summarize: In terms of the human beings' evolution, everything that's been built - call it civilization - well, the thing is you have to remember that it's all a recent development. The human mind, it's quite recent. Only 20, 000 or so years since abstract thought kicked in. You know, mathematics, art, and science. Civilization: granaries, cities, Chase Manhattan Banks and shopping malls. It's recent. And there's no going back. The good ol' days might live on for a while. In fact they almost need to live on in us. We are composed of these old memories. Religion is in our genes. Glory to the archetypal memories of gods and minotaurs.

Some of those Bible stories are pretty good, I gotta admit it. But there's no going back. That's the point here. The human race down there will just have to move on. Get smart. All that old-time religion stuff isn't doing anybody any good anymore.

And they're evolving at such a break-neck pace. Evolving quickly genetically because the gene pools mix so fast now. But even more so, they're evolving culturally. Hurtling down that highway of doom. Or is that just the road to Las Vegas I see?

The dragon, the corporate military-industrial complex, has been unbridled and unleashed; and it is destructive by its very nature. Yet the dragon comes from us, it is part of us, and perhaps we can stop the dragon/machine before it rolls over all the earth. People could well have sufficient consciousness to come to their senses in time.

But overall, from the vantage point of a phantom, it's the wonder of the human species, their courage, their optimism, their grace at last discovered - well, ya just gotta love it. Hats off to mankind.

Are they gonna destroy themselves? I doubt it. After all, the human species is one variegated collection of clever and resilient bastards. But what will the earth be like for the humans of the next generation or two? Twenty billion of them stuck in traffic jams, heat waves, floods, typhoons, droughts, famines, diseases, and televised fear. Without much in the way of forests or wildlife. Well, I guess we'll find out how it all turns out. As I said, I'm not putting any heavy money in either direction.

This is your phantom, signing out.

Zee Phantom

P.S. A final word: End

July 14, 2011

## Howard Makes an Entry

If any of you were possibly enjoying these little notes and observations of the Phantom, well then, I'm sorry to inform you right now that there won't be any more of these *Observations of a Phantom* for a while.

Attached to the last installment of notes (actually it was scotched taped onto the notebook cover) was the following letter:

*July 4, 2011*

*Dear Howard,*

*I hope you will get these notes published because they are meant as an addendum to the previous book, One Life or the Lives of Chester Knowles - which Chester had the Baum character write for him.*

82

*The reason I'm stopping is that I noticed in a fit of introspection that this phantom was beginning to run out of clever and fantastic things to say. I kind of pretty much said it all. I mean, I covered contemporary American culture and politics, whiskey and women, psychogenic philosophy and the associated barnyard noises. Also, old-time religion was covered, plus some sex, the midnight train to New Haven, and all stops in between. Whatever else could you think of? The evolution of the species and the hopes of humankind were covered in depth, or at least as deeply as this phantom would want to go. What more can a phantom say? And, as I have been explaining all along, being a phantom doesn't make me the source of any wisdom. So that's it.*

*Like the old folksong says:*

*Ya gotta walk that lonesome valley.*
*Ya gotta walk it for yourself.*
*Ain't nobody here can walk it for ya.*
*Ya gotta walk it by yourself.*

*So I leave it to you Howard, as well as to all the others, to go on with the story. This whole life, this* One Life *of ours, it's only a story. After all, we're fictional characters! Don't forget that.*

*P.S. It's also just like Hank Williams said:*

*"No matter how I struggle or strive*
*I'll never get out of this world alive."*

*Be well Howard,*
*And all my love,*

*The Phantom*

August 10, 2011

# Howard Continues

That's it. Those are the last notes, the last installment. To the best of my knowledge and in my considered opinion it does appear that this is finally going to be the last of them. Although with Chester and the Phantom you never can be too sure. Myself, I haven't decided where Chester begins and where the Phantom starts. Which came first? The chicken or the egg? Chester or the Phantom? It's all like One Life - which you don't need to remind me - was the title of this book in the first place. Personally, I feel thankful to be have been able to express my views and thoughts, and to share in this here Life (and Afterlife!) experience that Chester is creating for us fictional characters. And, as a fictional character, I just have to say that it's just very cool to be in print and to still be alive. I'm still struggling to figure everything out - which, I confess is something I can't stop doing. I suppose I am a continuation of Chester in that respect, which gives me a sort of role to play in this drama, or story, or saga or whatever it is.

I'm going to give these notes to Willie. I think writing and continuing Chester's story will be a good thing for him to do too. It's sort of a hunch of mine, a very strong hunch of mine, that Willie is connected to Chester more than any of us. You ask how fictional characters like myself can get hunches? Well, why not? Why shouldn't we get hunches? Actually, as a point of fact, Natale told me the other day (I must interject here that we (we meaning Andrea and myself) have recently renewed our friendship with Natale. Actually she and Andrea had this big reconciliation scene out in Vegas at the New York New York restaurant plaza that I won't go into. So long story short, they made up). Anywaze, what Natale said to me over the phone last night was that she thinks Willie and Chester are connected via astral connections. I believe that was the term she used, astral connections. There was also something about low-intensity beams of light. Natale asked me to set up a meeting between her and Willie, which may be possible soon because they both of them visit LA pretty frequently of late. In any case, I'm going to give these notes to Willie tomorrow.

August 24, 2011

# Willie's Turn

Howard handed me these notes. Again. And he told me in this emotional voice that I "really oughta" continue them. "Keep it going," he said. He also said that it would be like a "continuation of Chester", or something like that. I can never quite figure out what Howard is saying, most of the time anyhoo. I tell ya though, the kid plays a mean slide guitar. He can play with us anytime. And in fact he sometimes does. Actually fairly often. Howard still does play the guitar with us - whenever he gets out to Arizona, or whenever we stop by in L.A. Anyhow, as I was sayin', we just like the kid.

But back to business: Since I have no way of being able to clarify or explanify anything about any of the above notes, the so-called Observations of a Phantom or whatever it is he's calling himself, all I can try to do here is to "keep it going" like Howard says.

I guess I'm just going to record things as they happen. You know, because you need somebody to keep something of an accurate and objective accounting of this story about

Chester Knowles.... And me...... And Tony too.... And all the rest of them I guess.

You have to understand that there are some serious issues in the fire for me personally here. Things that concern my very existence. Existential questions, like they say. But me? I'm the kind of guy that tends to sweep things under the rug most of the time. You know about that river in Africa? That's right. Denial, it's my M.O. Modus Oprah Winfrey. All the same, I try to keep things simple. I play my music, have a good time. But there are some serious questions here. I mean, am I me? Or am I just some kind of continuation of Chester? If so, who's this phantom dude? And how does it all work? And never mind that I'm a fictional character. It still has to make sense. Howard's right about that.

Apropos of these issues, and in regard to the above: the quandaries, the conundrums of life and afterlife, the Gordian knots of existence, and in particular the who done what to who kinds of questions, here is a tape of a recent conversation between Gene, Howard and myself about the subject. We were talking about these things last week and I just happened to have it recorded. So this would be what they used to call a transcript or maybe a transcription, and which I am typing up - on this here Macintosh computer.

# Conversation

8/15/2011

Gene: So? What do you say? You guys both read it. (Inaudible) So.... So what? So? What do you think? Is this Phantom guy really Chester? I mean, Willie, do you think he's who he says he is? Answer me Willie.......And right, Howard, I don't care what you think. That whole theory of yours about how everything has to be making sense and all. Forget about things makin' sense....(Inaudible)...

Willie: Well, Gene, like I was sayin', there's a lot there that does make sense and a lot there that doesn't make sense. And I personally agree that it has to make sense. Howard's right about that... So, I tell ya, I just don't know what to figure. I mean I just don't know.

Gene: Yeah, I know. Yeah. I know, my brother. It's a hard one to figure out. But you have to remember that there's a higher intelligence out there - maybe from another solar system - that's probably just visiting here like a tourist for a millennium or two, or perhaps from inside the earth's core. I mean who's making those crop circles? The problem is that we don't have direct access to this force. But it's out there. That's for sure. And the Lord moves in mysterious ways, as they say. And it's true. The Lord does move in mysterious ways. There are just a lot of things that we can't understand. Even this Phantom fella says that there are myriads or multiplicities or whatever of possibilities in this universe, not to mention the other universes that are out there too.

Howard: OK. So what are you saying, Gene?

Gene: So what I'm sayin' is that maybe Chester has gone off into a different realm or universe. I mean it still could be that the FBI got him. Although now I'm not too sure about that hypothesis. Because if the FBI were really using or controlling Chester, why would they give us - and we're his friends after all - all these notes? That wouldn't make sense at all...

Willie: Well, I don't know about all your FBI conspiracy or the foreign universes in the core of the earth stuff... Say, you sure you read this thing, Gene?

Howard: Yeah Gene. You sure you read it?

Gene: Yeah, I read it. And I tell ya. It's not like Chester to play around with us. It ain't Chester to be doing all these tricks. At least it ain't Chester any more.

Howard: You guys are missing something. Like...

Gene: Like what?

Howard: Like this: Like why would the Phantom - whoever he is - be quoting Hank Williams?

Willie: That's easy, Howard. That's 'cause Hank Williams is up there in heaven or someplace in the outer reaches, I'll betcha, too. 'Cause where else would Hank be? And actually, it's also by a bit of personal revelation and inspiration that I happen to know that Hank really is out there singin' for the angels in the Country-Western Hall of Fame Cavalcade. That's where Hank is. And - if you like - that's where Chester is too. That is, whenever he's not out there on the beach playing tricks on Howard and all. No offense, Howard. .... So what I'm saying is that I don't agree with you, Gene. Chester is not above playing tricks on us. Chester's a doggone trickster. You don't know him the way I do. You forget sometimes that I'm an actual continuation of Chester himself. So don't tell me about Chester and his tricks.

Howard: I guess you're both right. But you know ... Chester. I know Chester too. Chester saved my life... like fifteen years ago... back there when I was lost in Utah.... (Inaudible) ....But now for these notes to just appear... I tell you guys: whoever left these notes and observations for me to pick up on the beach was like... like....

Gene: Like a Phantom, eh Howard?

Willie: OK, enough. Let's try that one in D again. That Leadbelly song. Remember how it starts, Howard?

Howard: Yeah sure. You know, my grandmother used to sing this one to me.

### Irene Goodnight (by Hudie Ledbetter)

*Irene Goodnight*
*Irene Goodnight*
*Goodnight Irene, goodnight Irene*
*I'll see you in my dreams*

*Sometime I live in the country*

*Sometimes I live in town*

*Sometimes I take a notion*

*To jump in the river and drown*


*I asked your mother for your sweet hand*

*She told me that you were too young*

*I wish to Lord I'd never seen your face*

*Or that I never been born*


*Stop ramblin'. Stop gamblin'*

*Stop stayin' out late at night*

*Go home to your wife and family*

*Sit down by the fireside bright*


*Irene Goodnight*

*Irene Goodnight*

*Goodnight Irene, goodnight Irene*

*I'll see you in my dreams*

8/31/2011

## Willie Continues

OK, I guess it's only fair that I begin to tell about myself. And that I add my own observations on top of whatever nonsense that's already been written down and recorded here earlier on. Because if I really am a sort of continuation of the Chester Knowles story, then I'll just have to try my hand at this writing business too.

Let me say at the outset that I am not going to try to explain anything. I've never been much good at explaining things. I'll just try to record what goes on. Maybe, eventually, some of you will be able to arrive at some sort of a rational understanding, or come up with some kind of a logical explanation for what is going on here. Myself, I don't really bother with all that. I have a certain feeling for it, and that is sufficient. At least for me it's sufficient. Most people want more, and, from what I can tell, it's usually their misfortune to want so much. They want to understand everything. They want to have control, control of everything, all the time. It's a quote-unquote "control issue" kind of thing. And to my way of thinking, it's usually just a big waste of time and energy. So I suppose I'm sort of lucky that I'm the type of guy who doesn't really want to know or understand too much in this life. I know that might sound strange, but it's the truth.

My name, as you probably know, is William Miles Morton and I am a rock n' rollin', country pickin', guitar strummin', banjo pluckin', piano plunkin', keyboards, drums, whatever instrument you like actually kind of musician - who is a part of this world and doing the best he can just to get through it without making too much of a mess of things for everybody else. And if I can make some decent music while I'm here, well, all the better.

I have to say that my current life, this current phase of my life, kind of began for me when I encountered Chester Knowles. I mean I have a whole slew of childhood memories. I'm not a freak or anything. And I'm not a phantom like some people I know, just kidding. I was born in a small town in Colorado called _____. None of my folks, none of my people are there anymore. They all moved out. The entire town just kind of emptied out. It's almost like a ghost town now. It's sad. But back then it was very nice. It was a nice place to grow up. We had a lot of fun back then, too. I was never too much at school, not exactly what you'd call an A student, but overall school wasn't too bad. As I say we had lots of fun overall. My brother Charlie and I would play baseball all the summer through. All day long we would hit them out, sometimes we'd have a real game when there were enough kids. We would be out there on the big sunny field, in the public park near center of town. We played guitar when we were young too. We're a musical family. Our mom played piano when she got the chance - which wasn't very often, though. She was always so busy raising us kids, as well as taking care of our Aunt Caroline, who lived with us until she died. My Dad left us when I was real little. But we got on OK. Like I say, it wasn't bad. I have pleasant memories for the most part.

But this current life that I am in - as Willie Miles Morton - this is clearly something else, and it's also clearly a piece of Chester. And a piece of Tony Santos, too. I can't explain it, but I know it's true.

I guess I ought to tell you about Marsha and the girls. The girls are big now. Vicki is 22 and Lori is 19. They grew up just like Chester said they would. They are beautiful young women. They still both live with Marsha and her second husband, Rick. Yeah, Marsha married again a couple of years after Chester "died". To a very nice guy. It's hard to think or say anything bad about Rick. He's a good guy. He plays a very decent piano, too. He's been a good father to the girls in his way. The girls know that Chester was their Dad and they remember him. Everything's really OK. The girls still love and remember Chester. And they accepted Rick as their Dad as well. Marsha handled the whole second marriage situation very well, with grace you could say. I suppose you could also say that I lent a hand there too, because I helped her out quite a bit back then - that is when Chester died the second time.

I tell ya, Marsha was confused at first by my name, though. That's because Chester had used the name Willie Morton too. But after a while she just got used to being confused - just like the rest of us. But about a year after Chester died the second time, I stopped visiting. I just keep in touch now by the occasional card or email. I did see both of the girls' high school and college graduations, though. Uncle Will hid in the back of the auditorium.

Now, I already told you that Howard married Andrea. Sometimes things work out well. They have a house and two kids in Los Angeles and they're doing really well. They did have some trouble about a year ago with Natale, which I suppose I ought to mention, because it's important to the story. I tell ya, that Natale, she's really a firecracker.

Anyhow there were some problems with money, and I guess there almost always are problems with money. I don't know exactly what happened, really. I never seem to know too many details about that aspect of things, the money business like I said. I believe I mentioned earlier that Natale had been in some kind of legal troubles. Gene even read me a couple of articles from the newspaper at the time, which was maybe like four years ago. So, to cut to the chase, or to get to the wind-up as old Davie used to say, she had borrowed some money from Howard and Andrea.

Well, you know Natale and Andrea have always had this thing going for each other. So, what happened was that there was a bit of a falling out. I mean now they're talking again, but at the time I'm referring to they had a falling out. I know all this because I happened to be there at Howard's house last summer along with Milton and Gene when Natale and Andrea were going at it, screamin' and a fussin' in the other room. We guys were playing acoustic in the den.

I only saw Natale as she was leaving. Our eyes met briefly. It was strange. It was like she was floating across the room on a wisp of wind. I tell you, that girl, that woman, is really something. Anyway, she was out the door real quick.

It's funny how you remember certain things. The way our eyes met. I think maybe the Phantom is right when he says that everything in this life is like a dream. Actually, I don't think he ever said that, at least not in so many words. So it's me that's saying it. It's all a dream, all the word's a stage, I think Shakespeare said that, and who are we to be so smart and think we can understand every twist and turn on the highway?

So, there you have it. Natale went back to Vegas without getting an additional loan from Andrea. Apparently she's starting up yet another business. Now, the other day, Howard said that Natale wants to meet me, to talk with me. In couple of weeks Natale will be back in LA, and so will we - me and the guys that is. So, maybe we'll have dinner or something. I'll report back to you then.

Respectfully,

Willie Miles

Sept 14, 2001

# Howard Speaks

Well, OK. There you have it. The notes up to the present point in time. The Observations, the One Life, the Never-Ending Story, or whatever you want to call it. Actually, I thought it was coming along just fine. In particular, I thought Willie was doing a bang-up job on the writing, especially for a fictional character. And I think the story was starting to get a bit interesting. But now Chester and the Phantom have thrown me another curve ball, and I need to interrupt Willie and change gears here. I'm sorry for the interruption, but it's something that I have to do, a duty that was thrust upon me, you might say.

You have to understand that I myself had actually been thinking that we - we fictional characters, I mean - well, we were done with a certain phase of our lives. That we had moved on, and that we had come to what Natale calls closure. I mean in regard to the "Chester vs. the Phantom" business at least. It was over. And we were going on with our lives. As you know, several months earlier, I had received what was supposed to be the final parcel, the last installment of notes. We were going on with the story on our own, completing things, tying it all up, moving on, etc., etc...

Anyhow, two days ago I received the following package or envelope............

Again, I had pulled my car up along the shoulder of the PCH and parked it overlooking the beach. It was in the late afternoon and it was on a whim once again. Anyhow, I went down to the beach. And I was drawn, I must confess, to the same spot on the beach where the Phantom had left his previous parcels. I was still curious I guess. Curious I guess about how he had done it. About how the notes were physically placed so close to the water's edge without getting wet - and more mysteriously, without any footprints or any sign of anyone or any thing nearby.

It was quiet on the beach. It had been a cloudy day, but it had turned sunny late in the afternoon, which is something that happens quite frequently in California. Anyhow, there it was, doggonit. There on the damp sand - right near the water's edge - sat a large manilla envelope. Inside it, as I found out later (I only opened the envelope when I got home), were several sheets of paper that were typed, but not stapled or bound together in any way, and which were faced front and back by two sheets of grey cardboard, that's all.

The moment I saw the envelope laying there on the sand I quickly looked around to see who could have left it. I saw some children playing harmlessly in the sand and also two groups of adults stretched out lazily on their blankets and beach chairs. But they were several hundred feet away. Anyway, I walked over, picked up the envelope and held it in my hands. I didn't open it. Instead I tucked it under my arm and walked along the beach for a while. Actually, I walked for a long time. I returned to my car as the sun was setting. I turned again for a last time to look at the ocean - all shining with a gold light shimmering and flickering. And I thought of my friend Chester, good ol' Chester. I thought about how he always used to say that he liked the beach so much. Me coming from Minnesota, Chester always was telling me about the ocean, how large and wonderful it was. Well, just then a pod of dolphins, four or five at least, surfaced and rose out of the water arching their bodies in that beautiful way that they have - and then smoothly re-entering the dark green waters again. Slowly they made their way up the shoreline. Nice and easy. But so graceful. It's something you see quite often on the beach, but each time it's something special.

Anyway, here is the entry that Chester is officially making into this collection of notes. They were typed on standard $8^{1/2}$ x 11 paper, as I said. My opinion is that this is truly Chester talking. I really think that all these notes truly do come from Chester. Which leaves us with the question of who the Phantom character is and what he is up to. In any case, the how's and why's of this story, the underlying explanation... well, it's still very much beyond my human capacity to comprehend. After all, I'm just a fictional character - just like the rest of them. All the same and nonetheless, I do not relent in my insistence that it make sense. I insist on it making sense. It's just one of my principles.

Well, you read it. See if it makes any sense to you.

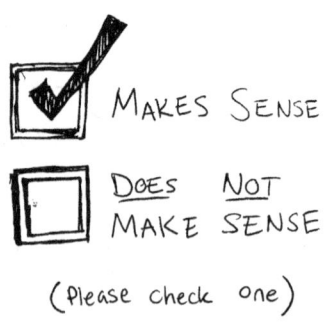

MAKES SENSE

DOES NOT MAKE SENSE

(Please check one)

# Chester Speaks

I know. A little explanation is in order. Howard is right.
I'm aware this Phantom character has been talking to you,
saying all kinds of nonsense. Well, he can't help it. That's his
nature. It's also in his nature to induce all kinds of trouble -
for me at least. He's an unrepentant troublemaker, that's
what he is. Well, to get to the point, there's been some
confusion, to say the least, as to where I end physically and
where the Phantom begins spiritually. And vice versa I
suppose.

Truly it is quite a confusing state of affairs. I'm still
working on it myself.

But let's start with the facts: I, my self, am alive again.
"I think therefore I am" said Descartes. And he set out from
that one point, and he created... well, whatever he created. It
is a fact, though, in any case, that I woke up once again in a
motor lodge near the Giant Sequoia National Park - which I
suppose you could say is a coincidence, but I think not. Not
that I believe in fate or destiny or the ability to know what is

to come, but it surely cannot be a coincidence that I am up in the mountains again.

In the meantime I'm enjoying it all. Every moment that I am outside in the mountains I am joyful. I feel things cleanly and more accurately when I am surrounded by the wonder of the earth. I could go on and on about the beauty of the trees and hills. The power of beauty to elevate and educate a man is truly something amazing to me.

But to return to the Phantom business. I know that this may seem a bit glib but there are phantoms with a small p and Phantoms with a capital P.

A phantom (small p), after all, is just a piece of the spirit, the great spirit. That great spirit or entity that spans this great, round earth and moves all things. A Phantom (capital P) would also be such a phantom, a piece of the spirit as we all are. But a phantom that is somehow aware that he is a phantom. And thus can talk to you and wear a hat.

As I see it (and the Phantom and I are actually in agreement on this point) the opportunity to be alive is such a great one that the only thing to do when it presents itself is to run out and grab the bull by the horns, toss the fates to the winds, get all your ducks in order, shoot for the moon, swing for the seats, etc, etc, and so forth.

You know, I've started to talk a bit like the Phantom. You know, all these run-on sentences and strings of trite sayings, going on for too long...Well, you see what I mean. Soon I'll make no sense at all.

So, I need to say good-bye, and in conclusion, I quote Groucho Marx, who said: "Hello, I must be going".

My best to Willie. Howard, please share this note and all these Phantom observations with him. Tell Willie he needs to figure out the Chester-Phantom business himself. Tell him he's the one that needs to come up with an explanation, an ending to the story. Because it's his story now. And tell him to keep playing that Country music. You too.

I'll leave it to you guys to finish this One Life story. As I was saying, I just need to grab this opportunity to be alive. Time to get off the bus.

All the best,

# The Phantom Speaks Again

OK, there you have it. Chester's last note, his good-bye letter. So be it.

I think I mentioned earlier that when our assigned person is managing well by his or herself, well, then, we phantoms can kinda meander around a bit. And that's the case in point here currently. I'm meandering again. Chester's just fine.

Not that we Phantoms float around on astral bodies, or anything like that. We have bodies and we eat hot dogs like the rest of you. It's only that - perhaps because of the fact that we've already died - we phantoms possess a deeper appreciation for the larger picture. You know, the whole enchilada: the eternal presence of a speechless and unseeable universe - never-ending in its vastness: the universe in which we exist, in which we are somehow alive.

110

For a brief moment in time, as in-the-flesh organic beings, we are alive. But soon we disappear, to return back to the dust, back to the soil. To Mother Earth. Eventually we revert to inorganic molecules, solitary atoms, the elementary particles, quarks, bosons, even photons, and we are scattered, borne by the galactic winds, to the far reaches of the evening sky.

So, like I say, why make such a big deal of everything? Just dig in to what's on your plate. Bon appetit.

*Nov 4, 2011*

# Willie Picks Up the Ball

Well, there you have it. Howard's returned the notes to me and asked me to keep on writing, to finish this sucker up. As for an explanation for all this reincarnation stuff - if that's what it is, and personally I doubt it - well, I'll do my best. I'm going to continue with the story. And that's to say I'm simply going to report what happens as accurately as I can.

Tomorrow night I'm going over with Gene and Milton to Howard's house in LA for dinner. Andrea is making supper. Andrea's a great cook by the way. She's inviting her friend Natale too, who I ought to tell you has kind of caught my eye again. Actually she called me last week saying how she has this crazy intuition about Chester, how he is alive again. Interesting, no? She hasn't read this diary or Observations of a Phantom notebook neither. What's causing all these intuitions and coincidences? Why does it always work like that? These are interesting questions, at least for us fictional characters they are. Anyhow, we'll all be meeting tomorrow night and then maybe we can get a better understanding on things at that point in time.

In the meantime, I'll share with you a conversation we guys had last week. Again, I had the machine rolling during one of our practice sessions, and this will be another transcript, transcribed and typed up verbatim, as they say, to the best of my typing ability.


## Transcript of Conversation


*(recorded on October 23, 2011 at Gene's apartment in Los Angeles)*

*Note: Howard had just shown us the notebook with the latest notes or letters he had found on the beach.*


*(Inaudible. Hear sounds of guitars playing in background, and then sounds of guitar cases closing. Music stops. Hear shuffling of feet)*


Howard: So Chester's really thrown us a curveball, huh?

Gene: Whattaya mean Chester? If anybody threw anything it was that Phantom…. And I say it was a fastball down the middle.

Willie: Just up to us to whack it out into the seats, right Gene?

Gene: That's right my brother.

Willie: OK, Gene, if that's the way you feel about it…. It's OK with you Howard?

Howard: Yeah, sure…. Sure, Willie…..Funny, though. Funny how the story seems to be coming to an end. I mean, here we are, all of us are just fictional characters. And all of us…well, some of us….are still trying to figure everything out……(Inaudible) ….. goofin' around…. (Inaudible)…. It's just interesting, that's what. Because if we weren't fictional characters, we wouldn't be anything. We never would have existed. These are just the cards we been dealt and….

Gene: That's right Howard.

Howard: Uh huh….Anyhow it's definitely feels like it's time to stop. All we need to do now with these notes is to finish them up. And Willie, you got your instructions….

Gene: Like in Mission Impossible……

Howard: Yeah, remember that show?..... Anyway, Willie, the notebook is yours just like Chester says, or the Phantom says, or whoever the hell, whatever…. To finish it up I mean. You finish it up. I'll still check down on the beach every now and then I suppose... Say, how 'bout we try that one that Chester used to like?

Gene: Which one's that?

Howard: You know. On that "Old Rock Pile with a Ball and Chain"…

Gene: You mean, "When I've Done My Time"?

Willie: Sure, that's a great one. What key, Howard?

Howard: G, I guess. Let's do it in G

Gene: We need a banjo and Earl Scruggs himself to do that one right, ya know.

Howard: Yeah, but let's do it anyway.

*On this old rock pile with this ball and chain*
*They call you by a number, not a name, Lord, Lord*
*Gotta do my time. Gotta do my time*
*With an aching heart and a troubled mind*

*When that old judge looked down and smiled*
*He said "I'll put you on that good road for a while"*
*Gotta do my time. Gotta do my time*
*With an aching heart and a troubled mind*

*You can hear my hammer. You can hear my song*
*Gonna sing it like John Henry all day long*
*Gotta do my time. Gotta do my time*
*With an aching heart and a troubled mind*

*It won't be long, just a few more days*
*Gonna settle down and quit my rowdy ways, Lord, Lord*

116

*With that gal of mine. With that gal of mine*

*She'll be waitin' for me*

*When I've done my time\**

\* When I've Done My Time by Charlie Monroe circa 1936

November 11, 2011

# Willie Resumes the Narrative

Well, I suppose I ought to tell you what happened last night at Andrea and Howard's, and we'll finish up this puppy with that. Well, we guys played our music for a while before dinner. We had a couple of beers as they say. Milton was acting a little crazy, but Gene finally calmed him down. At that point, just before we had dinner, Natale arrived. When she walked in the door everyone made a big fuss. She stepped in out of the rain - which had just started apparently - and her hair was all wet. I remember noticing how shiny and bright she looked. She brought two bottles of *Asti Spumante* as well as a bunch of flowers. As I said, it was raining out by this time, so her hair was all wet. She looked so beautiful. I wondered why she had never captivated me before. Because she did now. She even sat next to me at dinner. Well, I guess it just worked out that way, that we sat together. Well, we had a thing going before you could say Jack Robinson. Funny how things work out. But more of that later. As I said before, my purpose here is just to record the facts, and make sense of the Chester Knowles/Phantom/Tony/me story.

First let me tell you about dinner. Andrea cooked a goose with potatoes and greens and beans and salads, and all the trimmins. I tell ya' it was a delicious meal. We drank the Asti-Spumante. Natale, sitting next to me, radiated a light, a warmth, that I could almost feel. Like I could kind of melt right into it. Which I did, I guess.  Anyhow, we got along so fine the whole evening that we wound up spending the next couple of days together. Natale and I, in Los Angeles. And now, here in Las Vegas, we are together again.


Today is the 11th day of November in the year of 2011. A great day for the lovers of the palindrome. Gene also said that the next astrological age or something like that may be connected somehow to today's date, but I very much doubt that. I believe in just believing what you can see and what makes sense. But to finish up on that dinner, and also to return to the task at hand: recording things. And also, eventually, explaining things.

I want to return to that night last week when we had that dinner at Andrea's. As I said, it was a big dinner. Andrea's cousin from Holland was there, and a business partner at the restaurant, and of course the kids. And me and Gene and Milton. Howard of course. Anyway, after Howard put the kids to bed, we were still sitting around the table, just talking. And eventually the conversation gets around to you-know-who. That's right: Chester. Milton was the one who started the discussion. He said something to Andrea and Natale when they were standing together in the kitchen hallway. It was something like "All I ever hear about is this Chester…. You know, the guy that used to play like in our band?"

Natale bit for it. I couldn't stop her. She said:

"Why, what do you want to know?"

"Well, all I been hearing is stuff like Chester and the Phantom this. And Chester and the Phantom that. Like what's what?

I think I myself tried to interrupt and stop the conversation, but it was too late. Once Natale and Andrea heard about the Phantom business all hell broke loose, excuse the expression. It wound up with everybody ganging up on Howard, which I thought was funny. But Natale had become interested. Actually more like she became fascinated or obsessed. She was just dumbfounded at first - flabberbasted as old Davie used to say - by all she heard that night about Chester and Tony and the Phantom. She wanted so much to understand, poor thing. I guess that's also why I'm sort of destined to stay with her - at least until we get this whole Chester/ Phantom/ Willie thing sorted out. I mean I think I've got it now. It's clear in my mind what is happening. I just need to explain it to Natale and get her over this rough patch in her life. That's how I figure it. Excuse me. I did promise to just stick to the facts, just report what happened. Well, as I said, we had a heated discussion round the table, but after a while everyone calmed down and we had a quite enjoyable evening. Andrea served cake and tea. Like I say, everyone calmed down.

Ok, let me continue. And I'm going to sum it all up here. Chester is a phantom. He didn't know it at first, but now he does. Me, Willie, I'm the one that's still living, glory hallelujah. When I die, I guess the story will be over, unless I can think of some new kind of wrinkle in the cosmic order before then - which Gene says is entirely possible. Well, we'll see about that.

## Howard Sums It Up

OK, there you have it. I believe I have fulfilled my obligations to Mr. Chester Knowles, the Phantom, and to everybody else. I am having these notes published, as you can see. On behalf of all the fictional characters in this book I thank you for the opportunity to entertain you - if only for this little while.

*Howard*
*Hartman*

www.ingramcontent.com/pod-product-compliance
Lightning Source LLC
Chambersburg PA
CBHW070755120626
46557CB00002B/600